D0021309

By Gail Godwin

Ballantine Books • New York

Evenings
at Five

Gail Godwin

With illustrations by Frances Halsband

A Ballantine Book
Published by The Random House Ballantine Publishing
Group

Text copyright © 2003 by Gail Godwin
Illustrations copyright © 2003 by Frances Halsband

www.ballantinebooks.com

Library of Congress Cataloging-in-Publication Data is
available from the publisher upon request.

ISBN 0-345-46102-9

Text design by C. Linda Dingler

Manufactured in the United States of America

First Edition: April 2003

10   9   8   7   6   5   4   3   2   1

For

Robert Starer

Vienna, Austria, January 8, 1924–
Woodstock, New York, April 22, 2001

Evenings at Five

Rudy's chair

Chapter One

*F*ive o'clock sharp. *"Ponctualité est la politesse des rois"*: Rudy quoting his late father, a factory owner (textiles) in Vienna before the Nazis came. The Pope's phone call, followed by the grinding of the ice, a growling, workmanlike sound, a lot like Rudy's own sound, compliments of the GE model Rudy had picked out fourteen years ago when they built this house. *Gr-runnch, gr-runnch, grr-rr-runnch.* ("And look! It even has this tray you pull down to mix the drinks." Rudy retained the enthusiasms of childhood.) He built Christina's drink with loving precision after the Pope's call. Rudy did the high Polish voice, overlaid with an Italian accent: "Thees is John Paul. My cheeldren, eet is cocktail time."

Or sometimes Christina's study phone would not ring. Rudy simply emerged from his studio below and called brusquely up to her in his basso profundo: "Hello? The Pope just called. Are you ready for a drink?"

The ominous rolled *r*s on the "ready" and "drink": if you're not, you'd better be. I won't be here forever, you know.

The cavalier slosh of Bombay Sapphire (Rudy never measured) over the ice shards. The *fssst* as he loosened the seltzer cap and added the self-respecting splash that made her able to call it a gin and soda. Then, marching over to the sink: "I need Ralph." Ralph was their best serrated knife. The thinly cut slice of lime oozed fresh juice. Rudy cut well; he cut his own music paper, and he had been cutting Christina's hair exactly as she liked it for twenty-eight years. And in summer, a sprig of mint from the garden, a hairy, pungent variety given to them by the wife of a pianist who had recorded Rudy's music. Sometimes Rudy joined Christina in the gin and soda. Her financial man from Buffalo had given them two twelve-ounce tumblers with old-fashioned ticker tapes etched into the surfaces. She always kept them in the freezer, so they would frost up as soon as they hit the air.

Other times Rudy would say, "I need a Scotch tonight." That went into a different glass, a lovely cordial shape etched with grapes, given to him by the daughter of a pasha who had invited him to her houseboat parties in Cairo back in '42 and called him Harpo because his assignment in the Royal Air Force had been playing piano and harp to keep up troop morale. "I need a Scotch tonight" could mean either that his work had gone extremely well or that some unwelcome aspect of reality (his music publisher sending back sloppily edited orchestra parts, being put on hold by his health insurance provider,

being put on hold by anyone at all) had under-
mined his creative momentum.

"Thees is Il Papa calling from the Vatican.
Cheeldren, eet is cocktail time."

Christina was a cradle Episcopalian who had
gone to a Catholic school run by a French order
of nuns in North Carolina. Rudy was a non-
practicing Jew who had gone to a Catholic
Gymnasium in Vienna until age fourteen, when
the Nazis came. Rudy always liked to tell how
there were two Jews and one Protestant in his
class at the *Gymnasium,* "and the Protestant had
the worst of it by far." So Rudy and Christina
shared an affectionate fascination with Popes,
especially this one, with his hulking masculine
shoulders before they began to stoop, and his
nonstop traveling, and all the languages.

What did I think, that we had forever? Christina
asked herself, sipping the gin and soda she now
made for herself. Often Rudy had interrupted
himself in midsentence to explode at her: "You're
not listening!"

What was *I listening to? The ups and downs of*

my own day's momentum. We were both "ah-tists,"
as the real estate lady who sold us our first house pro-
nounced it. She herself had been married to an ah-tist.
Her husband's novel had been runner-up for the
Pulitzer, she told us, the year Anthony Adverse *won.*
Her name was Odette, as in Swann's downfall. Rudy
was fifty-two and I was thirty-nine and neither of us
knew, until Odette carefully explained it to us, that
you could buy a house without having all the money
to pay for it up front.

Christina would arrange herself on the black
leather sofa they had splurged on in their midlife
prosperity (a combined windfall of a bequest
from Rudy's late uncle in Lugano, with whom
Rudy had played chess, and a lucrative two-
book contract for Christina, in those bygone
days when there were enough competing pub-
lishers to run up the auction bid) and which the
Siamese cats had ruined within six months. She
would cross her ankles on the Turkish cushions
on top of the burled-wood coffee table and train
her myopic gaze on Rudy's long craggy face and
familiar form reassuringly present in his Stickley

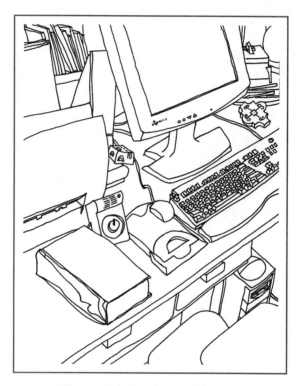

*Christina's desk with ragged thesaurus
and Rudy's metronome*

armchair on the other side of the fireplace. An editor had once told Rudy he looked like "a happy Beckett." Christina felt rich in her bounty: the workday was over and she had this powerful companion pulsing his attention at her, and her whole drink to go. They raised their cocktail glasses to each other.

"So what did you do today?" She usually jumped in first, knowing he would tend to her novelist's gripes or breakthroughs later.

"I finished the next movement of my piano sonata. If you like, I'll play it for you later. Oh, and I had a call from Henning. He wants to conduct the choral version of *Night Thoughts* in Boston."

"I didn't know you had a choral version of *Night Thoughts*."

"That's because you *don't listen to me.*"

"That's not a fair statement. It's just that I can't keep track of all your works—"

"I keep track of yours."

"Yeah, well, I only have ten novels and two story collections. You have *hundreds* of pieces.

Please don't ruin our evening. Tell me about Henning. That's wonderful he wants to do it in Boston."

"Yes. Maybe we'll go if I'm still here."

Rudy blew up quickly, but he blew over almost as quickly. Christina marinated her resentments, then simmered them over a low flame for days.

At other cocktail hours they would sit facing each other in silence on either side of the fireplace. (Two yards apart between his knees and hers: Christina had measured the distance after his death when she was wandering around taking inventories of all she missed about him.) They would sip their drinks and she would sigh and he would brood at her from under his eyebrows, until one of them asked: "What are you thinking?"

"I was thinking about my new book," she might say. "It's no good. I think it's died on me." And that might get them going for a whole evening, through a refill and then a bottle of wine with dinner, after which he would offer to read what she had so far. And she would creep upstairs and lie still in their bed and wait for his heavy tread on the stairs, and his shaggy head appearing round the door to say something like: "It's magnificent, it's going to be your best yet. But you've got to give Margaret a boyfriend— this is the twentieth century and she's twenty-one years old."

Or: "What are you thinking?" she would ask, breaking the silence first. Sometimes Rudy exploded with a tirade against toneless composers or a particular enemy. But most often he would look pensive and a little superior, as if he'd been called back from a place she couldn't go.

"I wasn't thinking. I was hearing music."

Freezer with gin reserves and ticker-tape glass

Chapter Two

*T*he gin was flavored with not the usual
one or two botanicals, but *ten*. Almonds
and lemon peel, from Spain; licorice, from
China; juniper berries and orris root, from Italy;
angelica root, from Saxony; coriander seeds, from
Morocco; cassia bark, from Indochina; cubeb
berries, from Java; grains of paradise, from West
Africa. International, like Rudy himself. Five
nationalities, but he refused to claim the German one ("That was forced on us when Austria

was invaded"). A gifted linguist, he spoke fluent German, Hebrew, English, Italian ("When I had my Fulbright, I wanted to see if I could learn a new language after forty; my teacher was pretty, she lived on the Piazza Mattei, across from the Fountain of Turtles"). He could get by socially in French when they traveled, and could erupt with impressive spurts of Russian and Arabic should the occasion arise.

He spoke a precise English, slightly British from his years in the Royal Air Force in Palestine. His foreign accent was not in the pronunciation of words but in his ornamental phrasings: even his recorded phone message danced with Rudy-ish melisma. He had a Shakespearean range of vocabulary and a richer command of American slang than Christina did. When a new situation called for it, he cobbled his own words: "the doctor removed two cancerettes from my face," "Christina, you are turning into a curmudgeoness." His after-lunch nap was his "tryst with Morphia," who dyed her hair a straw blond and drove up each day from New Jersey. His tempo markings ("creepily," "dreamily," "elegantly," "quite brittle," "exploring," "lackadaisical," "amorous," "relaxed with a bounce") were drolly precise.

He loved spoonerisms and his were top quality, often resonating with prophetic aftertones. His favorite, "The Cope palled," was a prime example. When the Pope stopped calling every evening at five, Christina's religious life took a turn for the worse. She no longer found assurance in the familiar churchly trappings. None of them provided compensation or explanation for what she had lost.

The Cope indeed had palled.

She and Rudy had started their life together in a two-hundred-year-old rented farmhouse in an upstate New York village chartered by Queen Anne. They sat in two orange plastic lawn chairs in the living room and put their glasses and the bottle of sherry on the deep window seat between them, until their ancient landlady dropped in one evening and saw the state of things and sent down two armchairs and a coffee table.

They drank Taylor's New York State sherry in those frugal days when they had thrown over everything but their work in order to be together: Rudy had left his ordered family life in Manhattan, and Christina had given up her tenure-track teaching job in Iowa. Rudy rented a not-very-good piano from a local dealer, and Christina typed on a shaky table found for ten dollars at a local antique store. The sherry was followed by a cheap Spanish wine at dinner. On one special occasion, Rudy dropped a bottle of Mouton-Cadet on the paved driveway of the farmhouse as he was getting out of the car. The image of his woeful face (childlike in its despair) as he surveyed the smashed bottle was graven on Christina's heart.

Now that Rudy was dead, Christina listened to him more closely than ever. There, the same two yards away from the cat-ravaged leather sofa (one of the cats had died young from heart failure), loomed his Stickley armchair. There was the tall Turkish pillow he used for propping up his back against chest pain. Only his kingly size was missing from the picture. The long face with the high forehead and thatch of white hair floated only in the gloaming of her memory.

But now, at the ghostly cocktail hours, she hung on his every echo. No need any longer for him to growl "You aren't listening!" because Christina was. Intensely. She heard everything that decorated his silences: the oil burner kicking in, the refrigerator (making more ice), a southbound jet gaining altitude after its Albany takeoff. The click of the surviving cat's toenails on the pine floors as he made his proprietary rounds.

"You *are* listening!" Rudy might now remark. And, always curious about her inner workings, he would want to know exactly what she heard.

"I was hearing," Christina spoke aloud to the empty chair, "something you might have said yourself. But first I have to tell you what led up to it. Remember, the last evening in your hospital room, you were sitting on the side of the bed, you were feeling much better, we expected they'd drain you and refuel you like the other

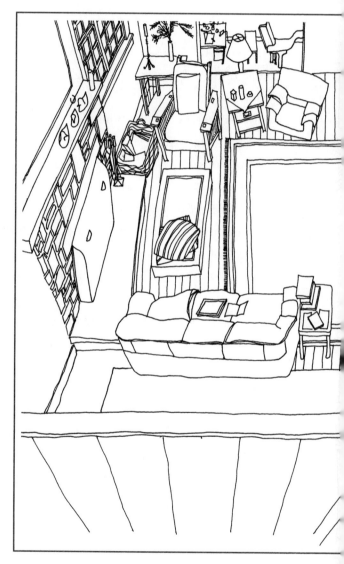

View of below from Christina's study

times and send you home in a day or two. You'd finished your dinner, eating the whole salad with French dressing, picking at the meat sauce and leaving the pasta, drinking the black coffee and spurning the red Jell-O with Reddi-wip. You'd been telling me about a passage you liked in the Muriel Spark novel you were reading, where she says if you want to lose weight, eat and drink the same as always, only half, and then adds that this advice is included in the price of the book. 'I liked that,' you said. Then I said I thought I would skip church tomorrow and come to the hospital early, and we agreed I should get home before dark. And I stood up and kissed you and said in a jokey-flirtatious way, 'Don't you dare leave me.' And you looked at me fiercely from under your shaggy brows and rumbled, 'We still have some more time together,' and I drove home reassured.

"Though of course we didn't. Next morning, I had to be content with saying farewell to your body in the hospital bed. But here's what I was hearing just now, in this voice I sometimes hear things. It's a wiser version of my own voice, and it was saying like a mantra: 'Absent in his presence, present in his absence.'

"And then I had this further idea. That somewhere in the gulf between those opposites, 'absence and presence' or 'presence and absence,' might lie the secret of eternal life."

"Or the secret of death."

Death had always fascinated Rudy far more than eternal life. Was that a Jewish thing?

"Or maybe," Christina went on addressing the chair, "it's all one and the same, only the order of opposites is reversed: absence in presence, or presence in absence. Depending on where you are on your journey."

"Would you like a little more?"

Christina could still hear the pitch of Rudy's voice asking this. Indulgent, protective, rumbly, but with no hint of a growl. What he was asking was: shall we continue this a little longer, this soul-to-soul cocktail hour we have built for ourselves over the years?

"Just a *little,* thank you." The happy reply of drinkers all over the world.

Rudy's ghost brought her the refill.

It was winter now and the wild wind screamed around the corners of the house they had built together in this Catskill hamlet fourteen years ago. "The Villa," "The Factory," or "The Orphanage," they called it, depending on their mood. Rudy had dreamed up the first two names, and Christina had contributed the third after her mother died.

"You are with me always." Christina continued talking to the chair, lifting the icy topped-off tumbler to her lips. "As in 'Lo, I am with you, always.' A strong personality comes into the world, touches some people, infuriates others, then goes out again. The absent one remains present to those people. Just as those people had their absent moments in his presence. Of course, nobody testified to all the times the disciples were fed up or bored out of their minds with Jesus. 'Why is he making us walk so far in this heat? Who does he think he is, why does he go on and on and then yell at us for not listening, why does he have to have such a short fuse?' "

And the wind whistled down the chimney, just like in the old stories.

In somebody else's story, Christina thought, the wind would whistle down the chimney, she would look up one evening, she would focus, focus, focus on the shadows in the Stickley chair, and suddenly *he* would materialize, sitting bolt upright against his Turkish pillow to ward off chest pain. Dickens could toss off such a mani-festation as easily as flipping a pancake, Henry James or Edith Wharton would finesse it with ambiguities, but this was Christina's story, and if she forced or finessed anything, she might miss the secret with her name on it.

Ralph the knife, with lime, mint, and ticker-tape glass

Chapter Three

Seven months had gone by. On the day of Rudy's April funeral some Jewish friends had given her a *yahrzeit* candle, to keep lit for the seven days of shiva. Now it was November and she took the empty red glass container with the Star of David to the local candle store and asked if it could be refilled and a new wick put in. No problem, they said.

The young rabbi who had conducted Rudy's funeral and burial with imagination and aplomb turned out to be a Jewish mystic. She told Christina that she would come every afternoon at five and sit shiva with her and help with the guests. And on the seventh evening, if Christina so desired, the rabbi would be glad to walk around the outside of the house with her and help dispatch Rudy's spirit on its transmigratory journey and then cook dinner for her. Christina said she was not ready to dispatch Rudy's spirit and that she thought she would like to be alone on the seventh evening. The rabbi took it sportingly and continued to show up at five each afternoon in her chic and original outfits. Trim little tweed suits with midcalf skirts, dashing scarves cleverly knotted, colored socks that matched her Guatemalan pillbox hats that served as feminine yarmulkes. She was tiny with long, slim feet, and wore different pairs of hand-sewn Italian lace-ups greatly admired by Christina and the friends who came to the shiva-salons for Rudy. The rabbi didn't proselytize, but shared her mystical lore if asked. She was a great asset at the five o'clock gatherings: artfully told first-person ghost stories are always a draw, and the rabbi told them well—how she finally had persuaded her beloved great-uncle to leave her kitchen on the fifth anniversary of his death, arranged a little ceremony, then opened a window and felt his unbound spirit take off like a freed hawk into the night. The dead little girl who had to instruct her mother through a dream that it was time to let go. Plus some Kabbalistic timetables of the spirit's itinerary, how long it lingers where, especially in the first year after death.

On the seventh day after Rudy's burial, Christina had been sitting alone on the ruined leather sofa with her gin, the spring sun pouring in at the exact spot where Rudy always had to shield his face at this time of year. She kept a sharp watch over the *yahrzeit* candle. It sputtered out at 7:43, and she stumbled tipsily out into the blue-green dusk, just in case Rudy's spirit was attempting a subtle getaway to spare her the wrenching pain.

A full-grown black bear was sitting with its

back to her on the lawn. Hearing her intake of breath, it rose with magnificent insouciance and loped off into the woods with its sleek high-bottomed gait.

And now it was November, and Christina, at first a faithful and then an increasingly immoderate observer of the ghostly cocktail hour (the 1.75-liter blue bottles with Queen Victoria's brooding three-quarter profile were replaced weekly now, with sometimes a 750-milliliter junior size in reserve in case she should run short on the weekends), was hours away from a nice little health scare.

Soon it would be seven months exactly from the April day when the undertakers lowered Rudy's coffin into the grave and the mourners formed two lines and took turns shoveling earth on the plain pine box with the Star of David on top.

In the Catskill hamlet where Rudy and Christina had settled, the artists (and their families or significant others) had their own cemetery. Odette, now resting there next to her

novelist husband, had told them about the "ah-
tists' cemetery" back in 1976 and encouraged
them to buy their plots right away, as space was
running out. They had procrastinated, of course,
and were saved only the day of Rudy's death by
a new couple from Christina's church who made
her a present of their two plots.

"Gil has decided he definitely does not want
to be buried next to his mother," the wife had
told Christina.

Five o'clock sharp. Completely dark in November. "Punctuality is the courtesy of kings":
Rudy always quoted his father's maxim in French
and then translated it for her, as if she might not
remember from time to time.

Secure that her full glass (lime but no mint in
the winter) with the ticker tape awaited her on
its cocktail napkin, Christina paced herself, light-
ing some candles. The *yahrzeit* one wasn't back
from the store yet. She walked to and fro across
the rugs, gazed up at the high ceiling, remem-
bered how they had stood like awed children
watching the great bluestone fireplace being laid,

stone by stone, by masons who knew what they were doing. Neither of them quite believed they were causing a house they had imagined for themselves to come into existence in the real world. And the builder and all the workmen took care of them like children, pointing out the advantages of having the house face southeast instead of northeast, tactfully suggesting that a bathroom door open not directly into the kitchen but into the hallway just outside.

"It's splendid, but are there enough closets?" Christina's literary agent asked when the house was being framed.

"Oh, Lord, closets," said Christina. "I guess we need some more."

Their one requirement, when the builder was making sketches, was that Rudy's studio would be downstairs on the northeast side of the house and Christina's study would be upstairs on the southwest side.

"I can't stand for anyone to overhear me composing," Rudy explained to the builder. "Even when they say they don't hear."

On some level of consciousness, Christina thought, *I must have heard all those years of Rudy's compositions forming themselves phrase by phrase, probably even note by note, but I told him the truth when I said I didn't hear, that I was scrunched into some dark soundproof chamber behind my eyeballs, straining for flashes of images that then had to have words matched to them. And he believed me because he had caught me not listening so many times. But then, later, when I heard something of his played at a concert, I could remember hearing it come into being. Sometimes I even had a visual memory of what the day had looked like outside my study window when he was downstairs in his studio plinking and plonking toward a certain sound and then suddenly bursting into a fully realized cascade of melody. And then the scrape of the piano bench, the transfer of his body* (thur–rump) *into his leather desk chair, followed by alternating solos of metronome and electric eraser. I heard without knowing I was hearing all the outer sounds of a work being captured.*

She switched on the lamp, sank into the clawed leather with a sigh, crossed her ankles on

Bathroom outside kitchen

the pillows, and—still not yet reaching for the frosted glass—dipped into Rudy's 2001 At-a-Glance appointment diary, the only record of himself he kept.

This was the final one, with entries—doctors' appointments, upcoming concerts of his music, dating six months beyond his death. ("How I love being the only one on the program who still has a dash after his birth date," he always said at concerts when his music was played along with that of the classic composers.)

The other appointment diaries, dating back to 1973, the year they had moved in together, lay tumbled beside her on the sofa. Her stash of elliptic Rudy chronicles to carry her through coming nights. In earlier years, Aspen, Geneva, Tel Aviv, all their trips together, the final one being to Stockholm, and the faculty meetings, recording sessions, rehearsals, premieres, and then more and more doctors began to fill up the pages until the final ones looked like these:

10:00 Allis
2:00 Dr. Donnelly
C in NYC
10:00 Allis
11:30 Justine
3:00 Drugstore
11:00 Dr. Paolini
C in Chicago
11:00 Bud (shots)
10:00 Allis
3:30 Dr. Ladd
C in Washington
Cocktails Rosens NYET
Dr. Salzman? NYET
10:00 Allis
C home

Allis was the seventy-seven-year-old Norwegian nurse who came three times a week to give Rudy his Procrit injection and neck massage. She also stayed overnight when Christina was away on speaking engagements. Allis had spoiled the cat by letting him sleep with her and putting out a short personal glass of water for him on the night table so he wouldn't get his face caught in her tall one: a practice Christina now continued. The lovely Justine, a dancer, was Rudy's exercise therapist, although he couldn't do much, but he always came home feeling revived because he had a little crush on her. Dr. Donnelly was Rudy's oncologist and hematologist, Dr. Paolini was his kidney doctor, Dr. Ladd his cardiologist, Dr. Salzman his ophthalmologist. Bud was the surviving cat, now in his own seventies in cat years, and *nyet* ("no" in Russian) meant Rudy had canceled.

Christina leafed through the last appointment diary. Red ink was reserved for beginning or finishing a work ("Began *Job's Muses* in earnest. Finished *Epitaph for an Artist*. Finished *Insomnia*"). The only other entries inscribed in red were Rudy's transfusions or his chemo. Bone marrow biopsies and skeletal surveys got only black or blue ink. Christina herself ("C") had never rated Rudy's red ink. Ah-tists could be severe when it came to priorities. The longest of all of

Rudy's red-ink entries was in the 1997 At-a-Glance, during a week of chemo treatment for his multiple myeloma.

> Positive but not exuberant
> Resigned but not depressed
> Finished piano quintet

Did the adjectives refer to the mood of his quintet or to his state of mind that day? Now listening to the quintet more carefully than she ever had before—his most somber, but with glimmers of pure tranquillity—Christina concluded it was probably a conjunction of both.

She sipped her drink and thought of how she had been so eager to get home before dark when Rudy only had twelve more hours left in the world. She sipped and sobbed like a child. If only she had known, she would have stayed in his room till the ICU nurses kicked her out. If only she had stayed. But she had gone home and read a novel late into the night, imagining Rudy either asleep or reading his Muriel Spark.

Back in the kitchen for a refill—Bud had emerged from somewhere and was sitting expectantly in front of his dish—she felt a rush of affinity with Queen Victoria as she cradled the heavy blue 1.75-liter bottle and studied the monarch's gloomy countenance. Well, what did the queen have to smile about? Even though she continued to have his clothes laid out every evening, her beloved Albert was dead, and she was fat from all the state dinners, and what was left?

When Christina had lived in London in her twenties, she had gotten to know the servants' chef at Buckingham Palace. He'd taken her on a grand tour of the servants' wing and introduced her to his colleagues. One of them had told her that Queen Victoria's nightly bottle of Black Label had continued to be delivered to her quarters until 1956 because no one had thought to rescind the order.

The phone rang in Rudy's studio. After four rings, his voice, which a conservatory student once described as "an octave below God's," came on.

"This is Rudolf Geber. Please leave your name and number, and your call will be returned as soon as *pos*-sible."

"As soon as *pos*-sible" took a playful leap up the scale, ornamenting the concept of what was possible with typical Rudy-ish melisma.

Christina slugged back her drink, some of it spilling down her chin.

"Damn it, Rudy, you could probably materialize in that chair if you wanted to. So could you, God. I don't know why I bother with either of you. Damn you both, my heart is broken."

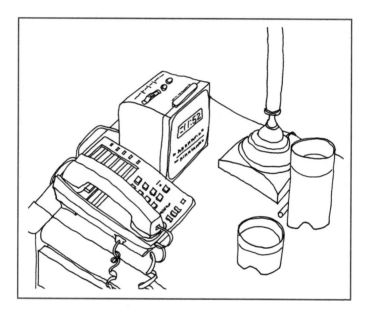

Christina's bedroom phone, with clock, cat's short glass,
and her tall glass

Chapter Four

⬛⬛⬛

*A*t some point she lurched up to bed, Bud weaving in front of her as they climbed the stairs.

"Don't cross *over* like that," Christina slurred irritably. "That's the way cat owners break legs."

The night was a horror. Dry mouth. Racing heart. Nausea. Dizziness. Ugly faces leered on the insides of her eyelids. Coming attractions of her future, perhaps near future, played themselves out. Who was that old novelist who fell in the toilet when she got drunk, and her faithless young protégé spared no details in his popular memoir after her death? Christina thrashed around in what was left of the king-size space, Rudy's former half being littered with books and papers, until Bud got disgusted with rearranging himself and went downstairs in a huff. Each time she dozed off she was awakened by ringing in her ears or stabbing in her eyeballs or after-images of flashing lights, as if someone had been taking nonstop pictures of her while she slept. For the tenth or twelfth time that night she checked the digital green numbers on the bed-side clock.

Only this time there were no numbers, just a watery green blob. She sat up and turned on the lamp. Everything in the room, even the precise English landscape paintings on the wall three feet away, swam behind a thick gluey scrim. Faint with fright, she made her way to the bath-room, holding on to things. The face in the mirror was so indistinct it didn't have eyes or a mouth. She sat on the toilet, head in hands, and planned the rest of her life. Learning Braille. Having to depend on others for rides, having to pretend to be a good sport. ("The worst thing, for Christina. Why couldn't it have been her hearing? But we can't choose those things, can we? And she's taking it so well.")

She could not bring herself to call 911, though she had done it five times for Rudy. The rescue squad certainly knew their way to the house, and she knew the drill: oxygen first, then the EKG, the questions, the radioing in to the ER, Rudy's deep voice behind the mask barking orders for Christina to pack his medicines from the kitchen shelf in the Ziploc bag that would accompany him to the hospital, calling them out with his magnificently rolled *r*'s: "Toprol, Procardia, Zestril . . . " She knew most of the squad members by name and where they worked in town.

On Rudy's final trip, six of them transported him out the door sitting bolt upright on the stretcher. "You look like Pharaoh being carried forth on his litter," Christina said, making him

Christina's bed

smile behind his mask as they bore his noble bulk to the waiting ambulance, its red lights already flashing. He told them he was feeling a little better already from the oxygen.

But now, crouched on the toilet, Christina knew she would not be rousing the jeweler and the IBM couple and the retired stockbroker from their beds or be summoning the young policemen from their night patrols. If the best of her life was over, she preferred to postpone facing it for a few more hours. She did go so far as to drag herself over to the sink and swallow an aspirin, remembering the TV commercial of the man collapsing on the tennis court and his son whipping out a Bayer. Then she felt her way back to bed and lay down and closed her eyes and breathed in and out, using the *ujjāyī* breath her yoga instructor had taught her.

By morning her sight was normal, and she went to church. Though the Cope had palled since Rudy's death, she continued to go because church was something she had grown up knowing how to do. And she looked forward to

Father Paul's extemporaneous sermons. Startling things sometimes came out of his mouth as he stood in the aisle in his alb and chasuble with no notes: "we just have to accept our inseparability from God" had been a recent one. Also the parishioners at St. Aidan's comprised the bulk of her social life. Important human dramas were in progress there: the retired sea captain who was losing his memory, the little boy fighting cancer, the lovely young teacher who had been proposed to by two men on the same day. Also, Christina liked to dress up, and today was her Sunday to read the epistle.

After church, the Mallows, the couple who had given Christina and Rudy their plots at the artists' cemetery, invited her to brunch and were so solicitous of her that she burst into tears and confided she might be going blind. They insisted on driving her to the emergency room. Gilbert told her about the time last summer he had been reading the paper and all of a sudden there were little colored explosions on the page. He drove himself to a specialist, who steadied his head in an apparatus and while telling him the plot of a novel flashed something at Gilbert's eye. "There, all fixed," the specialist said, having lasered together a retinal fissure. If necessary, the Mallows would be glad to drive Christina to the same specialist, even make the appointment for her. They remained with her in the ER all afternoon while she underwent tests. A CT scan ruled out a brain tumor. The doctor on duty guessed she had suffered a migraine and wrote her a prescription in case she felt another coming on. By then it was time for dinner and the Mallows took her to a fish restaurant by the river. Christina thanked them profusely all the way home.

"Oh, it was fun hanging out with you," Eve Mallow said.

Gilbert added, "When Rudy was alive, you two barricaded yourselves, which was understandable, with all his health problems. You were both formidable, though you seemed the more accessible of the two."

The idea of sharing Rudy's formidability did not displease Christina at all.

Rudy's medicine shelf

Chapter Five

*C*hristina's primary-care physician, Dr. Gray, sent her immediately to an eye doctor, young and thorough, who ruled out detached retinas and glaucoma but booked her for another kind of CT scan, because her left eye protruded and he wanted to check out whether anything was behind it. Meanwhile, Dr. Gray said, her blood pressure was way too high; this wasn't an easy time for her, he knew. What had she been doing in the evenings, how had she been coping? He had a way of looking at her as though he already knew, but he was a gent and let her confess in her own style. Because Christina liked her assignments in writing, he gave her a prescription slip on which he had printed in large block letters STOP ALL ALCO- HOL, and told her to report back in three weeks.

"And I wouldn't worry too much about the protruding eye. A lot of people have one eye that sticks out more than the other, but he's got to check it out. However, if you can't get your pressure down, we'll have to do something."

Back home, Christina took down the *New Yorker* cartoon that had enjoyed pride of place on their kitchen bulletin board long enough to have gone brown and curly at the edges. A couple sitting side by side on the sofa, drinks in hand. The man's free arm encircles the woman, who has kicked off her shoes and leans into his embrace. "I love these quiet evenings at home battling alcoholism," the woman is saying.

Christina tacked up Dr. Gray's block-lettered injunction in the vacant spot. She made herself a cranberry cider with crushed ice and seltzer and a carefully sliced circle of lime. Needing a ritual to signify her intention, she lugged the heavy blue gin bottle from its freezer home and poured its contents down the drain.

"Farewell, Your Majesty. It's time you completed your Scotland mourning and returned to your duties in London.

"*Arrivederci,* John Paul."

But she would not throw away the cartoon.

Now to get through the rest of the evening. She cleared out Rudy's medicines from the kitchen shelf to the left of the sink: the Lasix, the Toprol, the Procardia, the Zestril, the pain killers, the Nitrostat, chronicling in her memory what had led to what in the fifteen-year-long saga of Rudy's organs betraying one another and breaking down. The costly Procrit, still lying flat in the refrigerator, for when his kidneys, protesting the multiple myeloma, started to fail. She retraced the insidious transition, beginning in his sixties, when he went from being the one who dashed ahead up mountain trails and paused indulgently when she needed to stop and catch her breath until that sad afternoon when they were doing their back-and-forth walk across the flat causeway over the reservoir and he urged her to go on and finish alone: "I'll wait right here for your return." Off she went, while he sat on the causeway railing behind, keeping her in his sight. She walked quickly so she could reach the end faster and turn around and have him in her sight to walk back to again.

Dr. Gray had used the expression "blotto," which left less room to wriggle out of than the euphemisms she had grown up with. The lady who had spent the night under the piano at the country club in a pool of vomit had been tipsy. Dear Judge So-and-So, bless his heart, had been three sheets in the wind again.

The other word lately ascribed to her was

more flattering to ponder: Gilbert Mallow's calling her and Rudy "formidable."

Christina recalled the occasion last winter when the Mallows met Rudy. The local caterer, whom Rudy and Christina liked, was giving a small dinner party for his favorite customers. By then, Rudy was inking *nyet* all over his At-a-Glance diary, often as late as on the day of the appointment. Wasting time had become anathema to him. The prospect of being trapped in a boring gathering now triggered anxieties hitherto saved for being iced in on their hill or out of reach of 911. There was no bad weather forecast on the day of the party, but that morning Christina took the caterer's explicit directions and made a dry run to his house so Rudy would not be worrying all day that they might get lost after dark.

As always, they showed up punctually (*"Ponctualité est . . ."*), which meant they were the first to arrive. Rudy made his bows to the host, accepted a glass of champagne, and staked out a firm chair with an upright back. Christina sat

Rudy's desk and watch

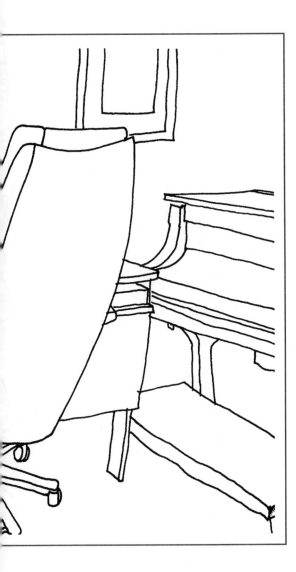

next to him. The other guests trickled in, among them the Mallows. Impressive hors d'oeuvres were passed in timely succession, champagne glasses almost too promptly refilled. A woman cornered Eve Mallow, recognizing her from the food co-op, and the two got into a conversation about the unusually large Brussels sprouts that year. Rudy smiled sourly at Christina and rolled his eyes. A few moments later he shot her a malevolent look, as if it were all her fault they were here, and rested his head against the chair back as if preparing to snooze.

"Please, please behave," Christina murmured, "I beg you." Gilbert Mallow, the only person sipping water in a champagne glass, was watching them with fascination.

"And their cabbages are also outstanding," Eve Mallow had to say just then.

Rudy sat bolt upright, and Christina felt herself lose control of his tight leash.

"An outstanding cabbage," said Rudy, pretending to address Christina alone, though he knew perfectly well that his basso profundo

voice could silence a room, "would be a wel-
come addition to this gathering."

She had hated him fervently at that moment,
so why was she now hooting with laughter until tears ran down her cheeks? The full force of
his presence was often too much for her, especially when he was unleashing himself on his
surroundings with that careless arrogance. But
now the absence of that force she could never
quite modify or control had left an excavation in
her life that cried out to be filled with his most
awful moments.

"It would be better to take a pill," Dr. Gray had
said, "than to get blotto every evening. Better
for your sleep patterns." He had given her a prescription for Ambien. "Start with half a pill and
if that doesn't work, take the other half."

Christina abstained brilliantly for the three
weeks until her next appointment. She had always responded well to a definite assignment.
She took one or two of the Ambiens, then

found herself falling asleep without them. When she went back to Dr. Gray, her blood pressure was normal and the CT scan results had come back negative and she had even lost four pounds.

But Dr. Gray looked sad and she told him so.

"I'm sad for you," he said. "I know some of what you must be feeling. My mother died ten years ago and I still miss her terribly. My father has never gotten over losing her. Tell me something: do you believe in an afterlife, that Rudy is up in heaven?"

"I did once, but I don't now," Christina admitted. "How about you?"

"I believe my mother's molecules are still part of the earth, and I know she lives on in me; she's with me every time I think of her," said Dr. Gray.

"I think of Rudy a lot," Christina said. "It sounds awful, but I pay more consistent attention to him now than I did when I had him right in front of me. I can hear exactly what he would say about so many things, the exact words and phrases and intonations. I must have absorbed a great deal of him in our years together."

Dr. Gray was watching her closely. "Look, Christina. Do you think you're going to make it through this?"

Christina considered a moment and replied honestly, "Yes, I think I am."

"We may never know what that blurred-vision episode was," Dr. Gray told her. "It could have been extreme hypertension. Or you may have passed a clot. Do you miss the alcohol?"

"Not desperately. I love the clarity, and I sleep better. But I'll probably have a glass of wine with friends over the holidays."

"Enjoy a glass with friends, but if I were you, I'd be very careful when you're at home alone" was Dr. Gray's parting advice.

Ralph the knife again

Chapter Six

Alcoholics Anonymous met at St. Aidan's on Tuesdays and Saturdays at five. Christina had often eavesdropped on them while weeding the church's perennial garden. If Rudy went along with her, he sat on a nearby bench, brooding fondly over her crouching form. Roars of applause erupted frequently from the open windows of the church hall. There was a certain exhibitionism about the proceedings, she and Rudy had agreed.

"The Pope will have left a message on the machine," Rudy would rumble complacently as they were driving home, about the same time that the AA group was having its coffee break, crushing out their cigarette butts in the newly weeded garden and hugging one another and tossing their Styrofoam cups and candy bar wrappers into the sand-filled clay urn the gardening committee had provided for their cigarette butts. Recently some abstainer had been taking out his rage on the folding metal chairs, bending them the wrong way till they broke, until Father Paul warned the group that if it didn't stop, they would have to meet elsewhere, as he was running out of chairs.

"I would rather die," Christina told Gilbert Mallow, who had stopped by to offer support at her newly abstemious cocktail hour while Eve was at the chiropractor's, "than stand up and give an accounting of myself to those people who stub their butts out in the church garden and abuse our poor chairs."

"There are more congenial groups," Gil told

her, sipping his herbal tea. "Or you may have the strength to go it alone. The one thing you cannot do, Christina, is make an exception—just that one little drinky-poo to get you through a party, the polite toast on someone's birthday. It's all over. Forever. Poison. You have to tell yourself that." In his eighteen years of sobriety, Gil had sampled many AA groups, from urbane Columbia professors to riverboat pilots (his favorite group), but now he walked. He walked in the country, but preferred the stimulation of populated streets. He and Eve kept a place in Manhattan, and sometimes he drove down to the city just to walk. "The rewards will be worth it, Christina. You'll find yourself getting words back. Whole rooms in your memory will open up." Gil had been, by his own admission, "a fall-down drunk," starting at age sixteen in prep school. Then when he was forty-nine he woke up one morning and couldn't tie his shoes. His first wife tied them for him and called a taxi, as he had also forgotten how to drive. When he got to his newspaper job, he couldn't connect the necessary mental circuits for laying out the pages. His paper had good benefits and he went off for six weeks to a renowned drying-out establishment and hadn't touched a drop since. Still, Christina resented being told *she* could never have another drop.

Gil brought photographs of his late mother's sculptures; he was preparing a major retrospective at a Soho gallery. Christina was very interested in Gertrude von Kohler Spezzi since she was going to be buried next to her in the artists' cemetery.

"It's hard to get the feel of my mother's work in these eight by tens," Gil said, lingering over each photograph. He sat next to Christina on the sofa, the hefty spiral portfolio resting on the coffee table with his cup of herbal tea and her cider and crushed ice with seltzer and lemon. At sixty-seven, he had smooth, childlike hands with almond-shaped nails gleaming with clear polish. The Italian stepfather, his favorite of Gertrude's husbands, had taught him the importance of manicures. Gil with his high sloping forehead, raisin-brown eyes, and neatly trimmed beard, who wore buttoned-up dark shirts and light-colored silk jackets, could have passed for a Mafia don himself, although his biological father had been an Anglican curate Gertrude had kept company with while studying stone reliefs in Romanesque churches in Sussex. "What is that funny-shaped vegetable on the altar?" Gertrude had asked Gil's father at his church's Harvest Festival. The curate, whose name Gertrude refused to share with her son, had replied, "It's a mallow," and so, back in Munich, when little swaddled Gil was presented to his mother in the lying-in hospital, Gertrude said he looked exactly like that funny mallow thing on the altar and put it down as his surname on the birth certificate. At this point, Gil's audience would express outrage or disbelief, and Gil would reward them with a sweet smile and say, "Wait, it gets worse."

Only, when Christina first heard the story, Rudy, seated directly across the long table from Gilbert Mallow at the caterer's dinner, had almost short-circuited things by rumbling, "Mallow? Isn't mallow a flower?"

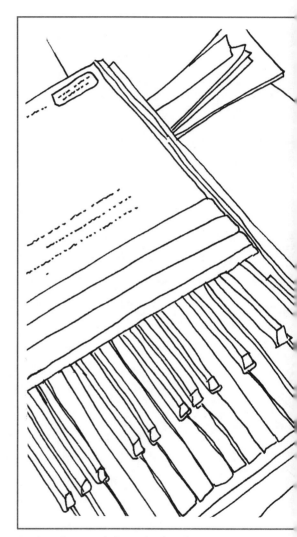

Rudy's phone and electric keyboard

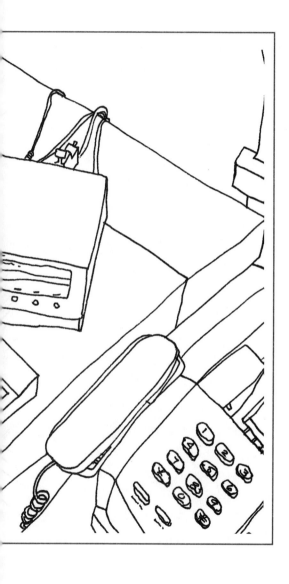

"That's exactly what I meant when I said it gets worse," Gil had adroitly countered, rescuing his story by making it seem as though Rudy had supplied him with the perfect transition. "It wasn't until years later, after my Jungian analyst told me I should try to relate to my surname in a symbolic way since my mother refused to divulge the identity of my father. When I couldn't find a mallow in any of the vegetable books, I finally confronted my mother. She was in her eighties by then and mad as hell because she had shrunk four inches and her stone figures loomed over her. She laughed when I told her about my research and then she said, 'Come to think of it, Bertie, he might have said marrow, a vegetable *marrow,* that's what the English call an overgrown zucchini. Also, as I recall, the curate had trouble pronouncing his *r*'s. *Marrow* might well have come out of his mouth as "mawwow," and I thought I heard *mallow.* I wasn't completely bilingual in those days, you see.' "

"That Gilbert Mallow, or Marrow, was quite entertaining," Rudy pronounced as Christina drove them home from the caterer's dinner, which, due to the seating arrangements, had not been a disaster after all. Thanks to the Mallows, Rudy, himself like a rotund but breakable sculpture strapped upright into his seat for safe transport, was completely satisfied with the evening. "She's pretty, no fool, either, despite the outstanding cabbages. Of course, she's southern. You southerners consider it a point of honor to be able to discourse gracefully on everything from cockroaches to cabbages. Quite a legume-y evening, wasn't it? What a gorgon Gilbert's mother was. I've known women like that. There's only one way to treat them: laugh at them and walk away."

"Unless they're your mother," said Christina.

"True. But they supply prime-rib material for their children to dine out on."

While Gil was making her a second cranberry cider and seltzer, Christina leafed ahead in the thick portfolio of Gertrude von Kohler Spezzi's life-size sculptures of women, if you could call them that. At the worshipful pace Gil was taking, they would never make it through the portfolio. If the figures were this disquieting flattened on eight-by-ten glossy pages, what would it be like to stand in front of a three-dimensional one that was nearly six feet high? There was almost a fourth dimension of malevolence. You were always being warned by museum guards not to touch the Henry Moores, whose generous figures made you want to cuddle up beside them, but Gertrude's football-shouldered, sharp-hipped Valkyries with their high, wide-spaced afterthoughts of breasts had their own built-in alarm system: touch me and turn to stone yourself, or see an analyst for the rest of your life.

I am going to be lying next to that person, thought Christina. *Actually I will be lying just below her on the slope, as Rudy lies below her third husband, Simon Newman.* (Gertrude had kept her second husband's name, Spezzi.) *Rudy and I will lie side by side, his earthworms visiting mine. I can hear his voice coming through the side of my coffin as it used to reverberate through a closed door.*

"Well, my love, how's your old girl today?"

"Too quiet," I might call back. "I'm worried. What if Gertrude's starting to get depressed about all the love she missed out on while working so hard on her art? She's more fun when she's malevolent. How's your old guy?"

"Ah, poor Si. He refuses to get over how Whitmore junior beat him up and Mrs. Whitmore defended her son, saying he wouldn't touch a Jew with a ten-foot pole."

"Well, but he's got his revenge," I would reply. "Look who's in the Whitmore family's faces now."

Magnus Whitmore was the notoriously anti-Semitic founder of the village's arts colony in the twenties. Magnus's grave, at the foot of the grassy slope, was topped off by an imposing six-foot Della Robbia bas-relief of the Madonna and child, with a stone bench on either side of her. But since the burials of Si and Gertrude and Rudy, the whole setup now appeared as though the Madonna was guarding *their* graves, which were directly in the line of her protective gaze. And whoever sat on Magnus's benches would look up the rising slope and contemplate the stones of Si and Gertrude and Rudy, and one day Christina.

Gil came back with Christina's nondrink. "Oh, you've been looking ahead. I can tell you a story about that piece. When my mother was working on it—we'd emigrated to New York by then and I was home from my boarding school— in one of my pitiful bids for love I asked her why she hadn't just aborted me after her study trip in England. You know what she said? 'I didn't know there was anything wrong with me for six months.' She said she was always irregular from all her gymnastics as a girl, and when her body did begin to change shape after England she looked on it as an opportunity to experiment with more rounded forms in her work. She made dozens of plaster casts of her torso in the remaining months of pregnancy, but she said the results were too 'pudding-y' and she destroyed them. The subtext of that conversation was that in an artistic sense she *did* abort. But at least she credited me for saving her years of time. Because of me, she said, she found out early that roundness was to be avoided at all costs in her art. And then you know what she did? She took up her chisel and mallet and knelt down and started hollowing out the belly so that the pelvic bones would have those uncanny jutting edges so characteristic of her work."

Christina was imagining Gertrude von Kohler Spezzi's grimace of disgust as she applied cold wet plaster to her pregnant body. But wait a minute—who had knocked it off when it dried? However, she didn't think they had the time to go there, as Eve Mallow's chiropractor hour was almost up. And also, Christina was dying to be alone with Rudy, even though it was only the present-in-his-absence Rudy.

Rudy's downstairs study

Chapter Seven

*A*fter Gil had gone, Christina decided to tackle some more letters of condo- lence, still coming in after seven months. She had them arranged in piles on Rudy's downstairs bed. When Rudy could no longer climb stairs, he'd moved to the room they'd built in case Christina's mother had to come and live with them when she was very old, but she had made a premature exit in a car accident. Yet they still called it "Mother's room," even after Rudy had been sleeping down there for five years.

In the priority pile were the notes and letters that had been most instructive to Christina, either because they opened up new possibilities for her connection with Rudy after death or because they provided models for future condolence letters she would be writing to others. Her first prize, so far, in the possibility category went to a woman who had written:

> A widowed friend of mine told me recently that, in his experience, love operates at a higher frequency after the death of the partner, and so it's easier to get through.

First prize, so far, in the model category (say something that connects the influence of the departed with the future of the world) went to the wife of Dr. Gray:

> I remember several years ago at a concert I told Rudy about our daughter's early attempts

with the flute. He encouraged me to start her immediately with private lessons so she wouldn't develop bad habits. Beth is now on her way to becoming an accomplished musician. Had it not been for Rudy's prompting, I might not have acted so quickly.

Christina picked out a deserving note from another fiction writer, a woman who had been at Yaddo the summer Christina and Rudy met and set fire to their respective lives in order to be together.

The card, from the Metropolitan Museum of Art, was a reproduction of a page of Chinese characters from a T'ang dynasty album. It was called "Spiritual Flight Sutra."

Dear Christina,

This is a very late note to say how sorry I was to hear of Rudy's death. I remember the two of you at Yaddo in the summer of 1972, seeing you walk around the lake with your arms linked. You two were the romance of the summer. Such a loss must be hard to bear and you have my sympathy. I hope and pray you will soon be able to write again.

Christina took out a note card with her name engraved on it and covered the front and back of it in her slanty convent script, saying more than she had planned and having to write in the space up the sides.

Dear Lauren,

Thank you for your kind note. He was a big man and he leaves a big space. I miss having Bach played while I prepare dinner. You will be glad to hear I never stopped writing. It was what I did for twenty-eight years while he was making up music under the same roof and it is good to go up every morning and keep doing it, just as if he were still downstairs. I miss hearing his little bursts of melody and all the rest that goes with capturing it, but in a way I still do hear. Recently, I went looking for his metronome and was surprised to discover that it

Rudy's chair again

wasn't the wooden pyramid kind I'd thought, but a little quartz thing the size of a remote control garage opener. Now it lives on my desk next to my ragged old thesaurus and before I boot up my computer every morning I turn it on. It's still set at the tempo he left it on, his last workday in this house: 94, smack dab in the middle of andante. *Pock-pock-pock-pock*, like a lively heartbeat, with the little red light flashing. It's very comforting, and I sometimes feel I am purloining some of the pulsing energy of his music and his strong personality.

Perhaps she could handle one more deserving note. Oops, this one was six months old, from the student of Rudy's who gave him the brass elephant.

I was in the practice room one afternoon improvising a tune when my professor stuck his head in and said, "Young man, you'd do better to go up to the library and listen to some Beethoven." I went on improvising, though my spirits were dampened, and after a while Professor Geber stuck his head in the door and said in that unforgettable voice: "Try it in B-flat, it might work better." It did, and I transferred to his class. I am the one who gave him the brass elephant when he retired. He wrote me a letter I will always cherish, saying he kept it on his desk at home and every time he touched it he thought of me.

That one will have to wait a little longer, Christina thought, choking up. *I can't rise to it tonight.* Lauren's note had brought back their whole opening scene, like having time's tail whip you in the face.

Christina's study phone

Chapter Eight

*T*hat cold and rainy afternoon in June of 1972, cocktail time in the fifty-five-room mansion at Saratoga Springs. The artists in residence, in jeans or other studiedly funky getups, are gathered in the downstairs library, a fussy Victorian room with velvet furniture and novels by late-nineteenth-century popular authors and volumes of poetry by Henry Van Dyke. There's a lady celebrating her eighty-first birthday, a novelist who writes generational novels about

Jewish families in Brooklyn, and she's wearing a blue-and-white patterned dress and nice jewelry and has stocked the bar with bottles of Scotch, bourbon, gin, rum, and white wine, along with the appropriate mixers, so all can have their choice of libations. There are also little dishes of nuts and pretzels, set out by the octogenarian novelist, whose name is Zelda.

Christina, wearing brown strap sandals with stacked heels, bell-bottomed khaki jeans with a button fly, her grandmother's gold-and-seed-pearl pendant, shaped like a tiny grape cluster, hanging demurely on its fragile chain just below the V of her faded salmon-colored T-shirt, has arranged herself, mermaid style, on a velvet chaise longue the color of saffron, and sips a Scotch and water, trying to look like a reserved novelist shrewdly summing people up. She celebrated her thirty-fifth birthday (prime rib and two beers) three evenings before at a Ramada Inn in Erie, Pennsylvania, en route to this artists' retreat, where she has been invited to stay for two full months. On the door of her motel room was a decal of a smiling masked thief tip-toeing away with a bag over his shoulder: PLEASE DO NOT LEAVE VALUABLES IN CAR.

Although she was exhausted from her all-day drive from Iowa City, where she was on tenure track at the university, she dragged herself out to her blue 1970 Mustang, the car she would still be dreaming about as her ur-car thirty years later, and unloaded the rest of her valuables: her blue IBM Selectric (which she would belt into the Mustang's bucket seat on the passenger side and drive off with in high dudgeon every time she and Rudy had a big fight for the next ten years, until both machines were replaced and the fights got less dramatic); two months' worth of ribbons and correction tapes; her cheap typing paper and her two reams of twenty-pound bond; her *Webster's New World Dictionary, College Edition*; her brand-new hardbound *Roget's International Thesaurus, Third Edition* ("You look so happy with your purchase!" a professor's wife had called to Christina as she came out of Iowa Book and Supply, and Christina will often think of that woman in years to come when she's opening her taped-up, threadbare old standby to find a better word, or track down one she's forgotten).

Christina clinks the two ice cubes in her Scotch and water and sums up her fellow artists. Some are sweet but not very interesting; most, including herself, are still hungry strivers, a few, including a sneering nasal-voiced twelve-tone composer who told her melody was the enemy, are downright obnoxious. Only old Zelda seems secure in her bounty.

Since arriving at the mansion, Christina has written fifteen new pages on her novel about three generations of women. She is on page 149 of the book, part one, the grandmother's story. Part one takes place in 1905, only twelve years after this mansion was built. The scheming housekeeper who will marry the father and steal the two sisters' legacy has just walked in the door of the farmhouse, wearing her black bombazine dress and carrying her carpetbag. Christina will make herself finish this section, getting through the night the grandmother's sister runs away with the villain in a traveling melodrama passing through the southern mountain town. Then on to part two, the mother's story, though the author is dying to get to part three.

Years later, part one will exist only in typescript in the university archive where Christina has deposited her papers. Part two will never get written. While still at the mansion—Christina and Rudy having burned their bridges and made public their intentions (too public, according to the twelve-tone composer, who was reported to have added, "But the Chosen People work fast")—Christina will abandon the grandmother's and the mother's generations and start the book all over again in present time, writing in a different way: filling in and rounding out as she goes, attending to the sensibilities of the moment rather than trudging chronologically from preplanned point to point. While still at the mansion, Rudy will pack in his tongue-in-cheek attempts to outsmart the Boulez crowd and instead begin a major choral work of sweeping emotional grandeur based on William Blake's

The villa, the orphanage, the factory

"Four Zoas," to which Christina has introduced him. Before she has to leave the mansion to resume her teaching duties in Iowa, Rudy will have sketches of the first two songs to play for her: "It is an easy thing to triumph in the summer sun," and "O, Prince of Death, where art thou?" She will leave her volume (*The Poetry and Prose of William Blake*) behind with him in Saratoga Springs, and it is to reside on his shelves in the three houses they live in for the next twenty-eight years.

Toward the end of the cocktail hour, there is a sudden flurry in the library, a galvanizing of the room's molecules as a tall red-haired man blazes in like a brushfire.

"So, Zelda, what's new?" he demands in a voice lower than God's, and the old lady murmurs something confidentially in his ear as she turns away from the room to mix his drink. Just neat Scotch, he tells her, it's been an awful two days, he's been in Manhattan doing a recording session with a bunch of tone-deaf fools. ("There's a new writer here from Iowa" is what Zelda has murmured. "She's nice, though she poses a little.")

"That's the composer Rudolf Geber," says a novelist named Lauren, who has joined Christina on the velvet chaise longue. The twelve-tone composer, standing above the women, says in his snide nasal voice: "He's very arrogant."

Christina looks over to see if the arrogant composer in his yellow polo shirt with the glasses jammed in the pocket has overheard the remark. He's standing next to Zelda, looking straight at Christina from under his lowering shaggy eyebrows. ("I find you the most fascinating person I have ever met," he will tell her ten days hence, slapping at his and her mosquitoes with his free hand as they walk arm in arm around the lake, "and I've got a good notion to throw everything else out the window, except my work of course. It would be the intelligent thing to do, and I'm the sort to do it.")

At dinner, he sits down beside her and begins plying her with questions. His mind ranges all over the place like a searchlight, seeking out the corners where she usually has to play by herself. If arrogance is the refusal to squander yourself on the unpassionate and the unfascinating, then he is arrogant. But toward her there is a generosity of spirit she recognizes as rare, an attention that is larger than self-consciousness. The world around them is soon canceled, but nevertheless, after dinner, when he asks Christina to join him for a walk on the terrace, she feels something close to terror and says she has to go upstairs and work some more.

As she climbs the baronial staircase to her room, she can't resist looking back at him. He has opened the French doors and gone outside by himself. Back and forth he marches on the blustery terrace, as if he owns the place, red hair rippling in the wind, yellow shirt blazing through the gloaming, canvasing the lay of the land from under his shaggy brows.

It's as though he's known exactly the moment she will look back. With a sweeping motion of his arm, he is summoning her to change her mind and join him. She can see his mouth shaping the words: "Come out."

She manages a nervous wave and keeps climbing the stairs. Safe in her room, she brushes her teeth with a tingly spearmint toothpaste and settles down in her bed to read some more of *Daniel Deronda*. Eventually she turns out the light and falls asleep. She dreams that she is walking along a street with her present lover, the one who awaits her back in Iowa City. Suddenly she looks up and there is the arrogant red-haired composer, standing in an open upstairs window filled with green plants. He is motioning to her: "Come up."

"Sorry," she says to the lover. "I have to go."

Facing south at kitchen sink in morning

Chapter Nine

Christina wandered into Rudy's study and turned on his desk lamp. She trailed her fingers along his closed Yamaha grand (he had bought it the day after he watched Laurence Olivier's deathbed scene in *Brideshead Revisited*: "What am I waiting for? If not now, when?").

She sat down at his desk and stroked the cool flanks of the brass elephant, perusing the day's junk mail she had placed on Rudy's desk earlier, an indulgence she continued to allow herself (along with his recorded telephone message, which she could not bring herself to erase).

Today's mail that had not needed to be forwarded to Rudy's executor had included a letter from Verizon, with its priceless boast in red on the envelope: WE HAVE PULLED OUT ALL THE STOPS TO GET YOU TO COME BACK!

Christina gave an appreciative snort and slid the envelope beneath Rudy's Seiko watch, still on Daylight Saving Time from last April, and admired her arrangement. The composition of the two objects gave her a visceral satisfaction, perhaps akin to that experienced by her grave-neighbor-to-be, Gertrude von Kohler Spezzi, when she had scooped out another inch of belly from a stone torso.

Bud announced his return from the great beyond. He shot through the door when she opened it, and protested angrily when she didn't follow him to the kitchen but instead flung herself out into the freezing December evening.

"Ah, Christ, Rudy, enough is enough!" Christina yelled. "Verizon wants you back and so do I!"

A lonely dog answered from somewhere below. She returned to the house and lit some candles, humming a swatch of an unidentifiable hymn. She caught herself humming almost constantly now, as if to compensate for the abrupt withdrawal of music from her life.

She picked up the cat's dish, scraped off the dried food, rinsed it and placed it in the dishwasher, got a clean dish, opened a can of Salmon in Chunks for Feline Seniors, making a little pas de deux with Bud as he wound himself in and out of her legs.

Only after he had flattened his elegant tail and hunkered down to take nourishment did she genuflect on one knee and gaze beseechingly into the crannies of the wine rack.

A last bottle of Gigondas, placed there months ago by Rudy's living hand, suddenly materialized and nuzzled its neck into the welcoming curl of her fingers. ("Enjoy a glass of wine with friends," Dr. Gray had said, "but I'd be careful when you're home alone.")

No, it's not easy, my love, when you've outgrown or

outlived all your authority figures. But you're strong. I remember the time I picked up your hand in the coffee bar in Saratoga Springs. They were playing that popular tune stolen from the Mozart G-minor. We had just decided to set fire to the status quo and be together for the rest of our lives. "Your hand is astonishingly soft," I told you, "but the grip is like steel." You'll work it out, if I know you—you'll make your own rules. The Cope palled and now you'll invent your own rituals.

"Ah, Rudy, Rudy, Rudy."

Assuming he was the one being addressed, Bud answered with an upbeat Siamese syllable.

"You couldn't walk around the house anymore without stopping for breath, but you could still pop the cork on champagne and open a bottle of wine."

Bud vouchsafed another syllable and then segued into his "going out" command.

("Don't look at me like that. I want a decision on your part. Just make up your mind and I'll do whatever you ask. You want to sit there. All right."

Christina had been in her study one summer morning when Rudy's voice, an octave below God's, came floating up to her. He was standing

. . . the pasha's daughter's glass

at the front door, reasoning with Bud, who was deciding whether or not he wished to go out. She had snatched up a pencil and scribbled the words on the yellow pad beside her computer because of their quintessential Rudy-ness—she knew they would give her a pleasure and a pang to reread someday.)

Christina accompanied Bud back to the door and he swished out expectantly into the star-filled winter night.

Back in the kitchen, she reached into an uppermost corner of the cupboard and eased forward Rudy's cordial glass with the etched grapes, given to him by the pasha's daughter in Cairo. She drew forth its elegant shape, held it up to the light, then wiped it lovingly with a fresh dish towel, the way Father Paul wiped the chalice with the purificator after communion.

Across the street from Christina's childhood home had lived a reclusive old lady, all by herself, in a big ocher stuccoed house, half hidden by overgrown shrubs. Mrs. Carruthers. Mr. Carruthers had been dead longer than most people's memories. Sometime after five each evening, Mrs. Carruthers's middle-aged son, Freddie, who worked at the bank, would park his black Packard in his mother's driveway and dart behind the shrubbery carrying a brown paper bag twisted at the top. A half hour or so later he would emerge, carrying the same bag, twisted at the top, and drive away. Everyone knew what was in the bag and everyone knew the pact Mrs. Carruthers had made with her solitary life. The bag contained a bottle of wine. Inside the house, Freddie uncorked the bottle, measured exactly half of its contents into his father's old cut-glass decanter, poured his mother her first glass, and drove off with the recorked bottle to his own house, which he shared with another bachelor who worked in the library. The next evening, Freddie would arrive punctually and pour the rest of the previous day's bottle into the decanter. On the third evening he would bring a new bottle and start the process over again.

"Well, the sun has just set over the yardarm," Christina's mother would announce when Freddie's Packard pulled in across the street.

"Do you think they buy it for her by the case or what?" Christina's grandmother wondered.

"They certainly can't buy anything decent around here," Christina's mother would say. "They probably stock up when they go on their little trips to Atlanta."

Rudy had loved this story and often told it to people. He was fascinated by southern speech and manners and the secrets they covered up yet didn't cover up.

Christina measured exactly one full portion into Rudy's cordial glass. Then she recorked the Gigondas (which Rudy had chosen because it was called "Oratorio") and scrutinized its remaining level. Four evenings' worth, if she was careful. (This advice is included in the price of the story.)

"And then I'll go from there, creating my

own rituals. Taking possession, in nightly incre-
ments, of all you meant to me."

For the second time since Rudy's death,
Christina sat down in his magisterial Stickley
armchair on the other side of the fireplace.

Christina's sofa, Rudy's chair

Chapter Ten

*T*he first time in the chair had been back
in April, just after Christina had finished
with her seven days of shiva-salons and was
alone again in the evenings.

Father Paul and Eliza, a parishioner she especially liked, had showed up around five to see
how she was getting on, and after a few minutes
of warm, intelligent, dry-eyed conversation with
them, Christina found herself whooping and
wailing and totally out of control.

"I just wish I knew where he was," she managed to blurt between sobs.

"Have you prayed?" asked Father Paul.

"I'm not sure I can."

"Have you asked Rudy to help you?"

"No."

"Have you read the Burial Office?"

"No."

"Would you like to do that now?"

"Yes."

While Father Paul went out to his car to get his Bible and *The Book of Common Prayer*, Eliza snuggled up next to Christina on the sofa and wept with her like a sister in grief. A year ago Eliza had had to leave her dying father's bedside in England in order to fly home to her husband, who had just had a stroke.

"If only I had known it was our last night together," Christina choked out, "I would have stayed with him."

"I know, I know," said Eliza. "You wanted to be there. All this time you've been with him and you feel you let him down at the end. You feel like the disciples did about falling asleep in the garden."

"Where should I sit?" Christina asked Father Paul when he returned.

"Where would you like to sit?" he asked.

And that was when she chose Rudy's chair.

Father Paul dropped cross-legged to the floor like a yogi and spread his open books out on the altar of the coffee table. Eliza sat in the black leather chair, which, for some reason, unlike its matching sofa, had escaped the ravages of the cats.

"We'll take this slowly," said Father Paul, and waited while Christina went through another cycle of wild crying and gasping. While her body was succumbing to these paroxysms, her mind coolly registered how impatient she had been all her life and how she projected this impatience onto others: *Surely Eliza must be dying to get home to Jack, and Father Paul has had a long day and wishes I would pull myself together so we could get on with it and he could go home and have his supper.*

But Father Paul gave no signs of wanting to get

on with it. When he did begin reading the burial service and selections from scripture, it was in an alert, rather surprised way, as though he were coming upon the words himself for the first time.

It was new for Christina not to follow along in the prayer book, rushing ahead with her eyes. She allowed the words to pass over or soak into her as they saw fit.

Bud crouched solemnly on the rug, very much a part of the gathering. At one point, he arose, stretched sinuously, and ambled off to the kitchen, from where they could hear him slowly crunching his dry food. Presently, he returned and took up his former pose, a neatly folded cat.

"Hope that is seen is not hope," Father Paul read from Romans. "Why hope for what is already seen? But if we hope for what we do not see, we wait for it with eagerness and patience."

Now, on this December night early in the eighth month after Rudy's death, Christina, in his chair, raised his/her glass (what is the sound of one glass toasting?) and took a determined but rational sip of the Gigondas "Oratorio."

"To hope," she said, gazing at her own absent place on the sofa. "What did you see when I was sitting over there, two yards away from you?"

"I saw you, my love. In your varied manifestations. In your married vanifestations."

"I've missed you. There were things left un-finished. I thought we would have the summer together. You said, 'We still have some more time together.' Your last words to me. Did you really think so?"

"I hoped so."

"I went home and read a novel. I was never able to finish it afterward. It's not her fault, but I won't ever read that writer again. I read until two or three in the morning. You were sinking but I didn't know it. I'm glad you had Edward, the same nurse who was with you eleven Aprils ago when, as you put it, 'I made my maiden voyage to intensive care.'

"Edward said I could call him at home and he told me all I wanted to hear, which was everything. How delighted you were to see him when he came on duty. How you filled him in on the intervening years, our trip to Sweden for my book, the last time we traveled together, what you had been writing, the operas and musical plays we wrote together.

" 'But then,' you told him, 'my life slowly changed and I could do less and less.'

"Around ten, you had chest pains. The heart doctor ordered a drip of nitro and some morphine. You settled down and slept some. Toward morning, your oxygen started dropping, more diuretics were administered, a blood test showed dialysis was needed. Your kidney doctor was on vacation, so his associate came and you signed the papers. Then your blood pressure began to drop, your breathing got shallow, they administered more diuretics, and when the doctor was putting in the catheter for dialysis, your heart rate dropped and you lost consciousness: not enough oxygen to the brain, Edward explained. They called code blue, the crash cart came, all your numbers were sky high, the pH of your blood changed, and Edward and the other nurses realized at a certain point in the resuscitation that they had just lost you.

" 'We were devastated,' he said. 'We stood around the bed holding hands. We were in a daze. This man was affecting all of us. His energy was still there.'

" 'He's a man I'll never forget,' said Edward. 'I was surprised that a man so sick could maintain such a high level of consciousness right to the end.'

"You were conscious enough to bring your life story to completion, with Edward as the listener.

"At seven-thirty the phone woke me. I picked it up, expecting your rumbly voice, instructing me what to bring, sweater, socks, in case they were keeping you another day.

"But a stranger asked for me by name, and when I said, 'Speaking,' he identified himself as the doctor on duty at the ICU. 'I have bad news,' he said. 'Rudy didn't make it.'

" 'Do you mean he's dead?' For those few seconds I guess I was still clinging to the thinnest semantic thread: 'didn't make it' maybe meaning you'd lost consciousness or not responded, something just short of hopeless, but on this side of death.

"But no.

"Then I heard myself asking, 'Is it all right if I come and see him anyway?'

"When I got to the ICU, a nurse came out, weeping, and asked me to wait a few more minutes outside your room—four-fifteen—while she finished 'getting you ready.' I stood with my back to the nurses' station, facing your partially closed door, hugging my purse to my chest and reciting Hail Marys to regulate my breathing. I could catch glimpses of her moving efficiently back and forth from bed to sink to waste container, cleaning up after the crash cart exertions. Then she said I could come in.

"Your skin was still warm. Your cheeks and chin were stubbled with fresh growth and there was a bandage around your neck with a trace of dried blood. Your body in the blue-and-white patterned hospital gown was more rotund than

before, obviously swollen, as was your face,
which gave it the fullness of complacency.

"You weren't there, anybody could see that.
But you had left behind an expression of . . .
how to describe it? Superiority? Bemusement
beyond caring? A distanced, tranquil amuse-
ment? Satisfaction at a task completed?

"The nurse went out, and I touched your
face and then your hands, which could bring
forth such complicated sounds, and which, for
the first time, did not respond to my touch with
a squeeze or a grasp. I looked away, then back,
half expecting I could surprise you into a
change of expression.

"It was my first experience of looking at you
when I couldn't influence how you looked back
at me.

"Now I have to make the crossover between
image and presence. The funny thing is, I can
still *hear* the essential you, though I miss having
you in my sight. I, the visual one, now have to
rely on sounds."

Coda

I used to try to be original," you said about your
work, not long before you died. "Now I try to
be clear and essential."

About Bach, you remarked, at the end of a day
when you'd had another transfusion, "He has order
and stability, qualities one doesn't always have in one's
life. Yet he's not predictable, sentimental, or personal."

And then there was the night, in our last months
together, when I sat over there on the sofa and regaled

you at length about all my fears: about my work, about the future, about my fear of losing you.

Later, after I was upstairs in bed, and you were in one of your commutes between the refrigerator and a late movie in your study, you called up to me:

"Hello? Are you still awake?"

"Yes," I called back. "Why?"

"Bud is sitting right outside your door. He's protecting you from all evil and danger."